CANYONS

CANYONS

DON P. ROTHAUS

THE CHILD'S WORLD©, INC.

PHOTO CREDITS

TOM STACK & ASSOCIATES / Terry Donnelly: front cover *(Bryce Canyon, Utah)*
TOM STACK & ASSOCIATES / Rich Buzzelli: 2 *(Grand Canyon, Arizona)*
TOM STACK & ASSOCIATES / Spencer Swanger: 6
UNICORN STOCK PHOTOS / Marie Mills: 9
ERWIN C BUD NIELSON; 10, 24
UNICORN STOCK PHOTOS / H. Schmeiser: 13
TOM STACK & ASSOCIATES / Greg Vaughn: 15
BUD NORTON: 16, 19
TOM STACK & ASSOCIATES: 20
TOM STACK & ASSOCIATES / D. Holden Bailey: 23
TOM STACK & ASSOCIATES / John Shaw: 26
ROBERT FRIED: 29, 30

PHOTO RESEARCH

Jim Rothaus / James R. Rothaus & Associates

PHOTO EDITOR

Robert A. Honey / Seattle

Printed in the United States of America.

Rothaus, Don.
Canyons / Don P. Rothaus.
p.   cm.
Includes index.
ISBN 1-56766-322-2 (hc)
1. Canyons—Juvenile literature.   I. Title.
GB562.R68   1996
551.4'42—dc20   96-2721
                       CIP
                       AC

TABLE OF CONTENTS

The white water explodes over the top of your raft as the river guide steers through the rapids. The steep walls of rock on both sides of the river race by as you travel down nature's rollercoaster. As the last wave breaks across the raft, the river calms and your speed slows. The shadows, the colors, and the large rock formations draw eyes up the walls toward a sliver of sky. The beauty of this river is revealed.

⇐ **Steering a raft in the Grand Canyon requires a lot of skill.**

WHAT IS A CANYON?

A canyon is a long, deep, narrow valley with steep sides. In many canyons, the sides are so steep, they are almost straight up and down. Canyons often form in areas that have mountains. Sometimes they form in a *plateau*, a large, flat area that is higher than the surrounding land.

Many canyons have a river or stream at the bottom. That is because canyons are created by water. The water slowly wears its way down through the layers of rock. This wearing-away action is called *erosion*.

Water from Havasu Falls in Arizona is cutting a canyon. $\Rightarrow$

HOW DOES EROSION FORM A CANYON?

Running water can scrape and cut rock just like sandpaper smoothes rough wood or metal. The moving water and the tiny pieces of rock and dirt bounce against the bottom of the riverbed and break off more tiny pieces of rock. Erosion is faster when the water flows quickly or carries a lot of rock, sand, or soil. Even so, erosion is very slow. Forming a deep canyon takes millions of years!

⇐ **The signs of water erosion are clearly seen in Cork Screw Canyon, Arizona.**

THE GRAND CANYON

The most famous canyon in the United States is the Grand Canyon in northern Arizona. The walls of the Grand Canyon are about a mile high! At the bottom of the Grand Canyon is the Colorado River, which created this enormous valley. The canyon walls are a rainbow of colors when the sun strikes them. The sun brings out the orange, pink, yellow, green, and red of the canyon's many rock layers. Imagine how wondrous this canyon must have seemed to the first explorers.

Today, visitors can view the canyon from various places along its edge. More adventurous visitors can hike down into the canyon. Others prefer to see the canyon from the back of a mule as it slowly climbs down into the canyon.

Riding a mule to the bottom of the Grand Canyon is educational and fun. ⇒

THE DEEPEST CANYON IN THE UNITED STATES

The Snake River travels through four states before it flows into the Columbia River. At the border between Idaho and Oregon, the powerful Snake River has cut Hell's Canyon, the deepest canyon in the United States. Hell's Canyon is 125 miles long and almost 8,000 feet deep. The many national parks along the Snake River help protect the canyon and the plants and animals that live within it.

Pittsburg Landing is one of Hell's Canyon's camping and boat launching sites. ⇒

THE DEEPEST CANYON IN THE WORLD

The South American country of Peru has the two deepest canyons in the world. The Colca River has carved its way through the Andes Mountains to form the Colca Canyon. At 10,500 feet dep, the Colca Canyon is twice as deep as the Grand Canyon! The Colca River passes many villages that depend on its water for their fields. Not until 1981 did anyone travel down the Colca Canyon by raft or kayak. The canyon's dangerous rapids have caused many deaths.

⇐ **The Colca Canyon in Peru has ruins nearby that are older than the Incas.**   **17**

Peru's Cotahuasi River has created a canyon that is just as impressive. In fact, the Cotahuasi and Colca Canyons are so similar that people argue over which one is deeper. The National Geographic Institute of Peru believes that Cotahuasi is slightly deeper. Measuring the depth of such an enormous canyon is very difficult. Until everyone agrees how it should be done, the argument over the two canyons will continue.

The flowers on the rims of Colca and Cotahuasi Canyons add color to the land. ⇒

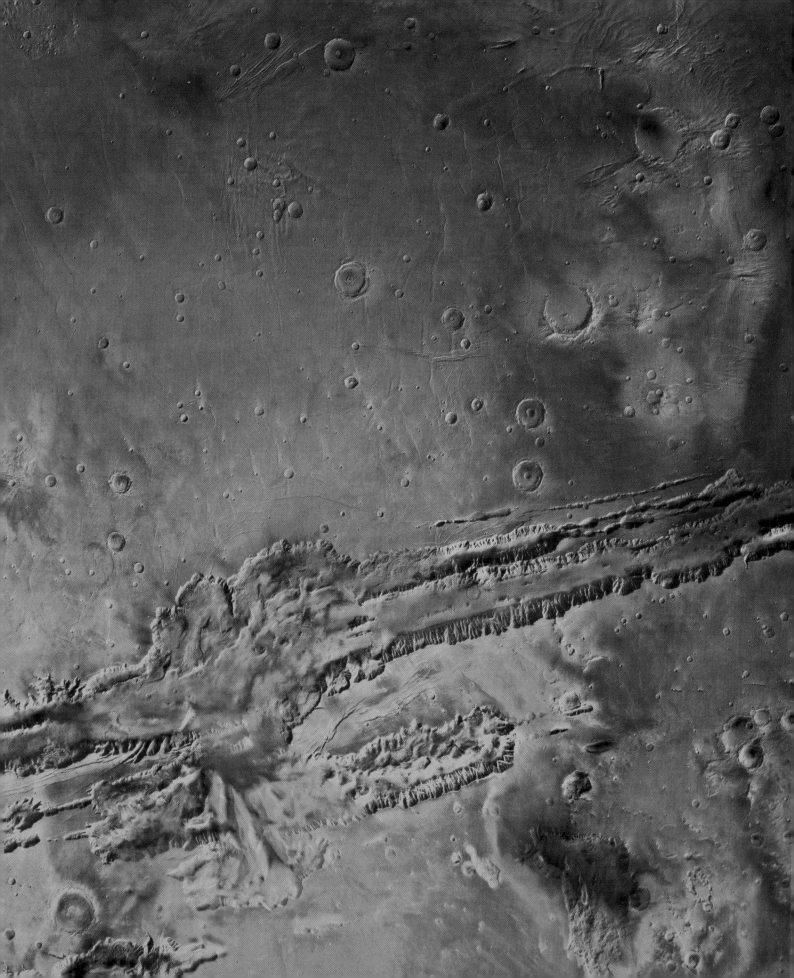

CANYONS OUT OF THIS WORLD

Earth is not the only place with canyons. They have also been seen on Mars, the fourth planet from the Sun in our solar system. Mars has the largest and deepest canyons known in our solar system. This system of canyons is known as the Valles Marineris. Stretching for 2,500 miles, the Valles Marineris are three to six miles deep! Unlike most of the canyons on earth, these Martian canyons do not have rivers or streams running through them. Millions of years ago, water erosion helped form these canyons. Today, however, Mars is as dry and barren as a desert.

⇐ **The land on both sides of Valles Marineris on Mars is pitted with huge craters.**

CANYONS IN THE OCEAN

Submarine canyons are deep valleys that have been cut into the floor of the ocean. Like canyons found on land, submarine canyons have very steep walls. These canyons are formed by underwater currents that are caused by earthquakes, tidal waves, and undersea landslides. Like an underwater river, the currents erode large areas of the ocean bottom. The deepest submarine canyons are found off the shore of large rivers like the Amazon, the Hudson, and the Mississippi.

A scuba diver is deep underwater between the cliffs of Black Rock Canyon. ⇒

Can you imagine climbing a tall ladder to your front door? Or pulling yourself up along a steep canyon wall to your living room? That is how the Native Americans known as the Anasazi lived. The Canyon de Chelly National Monument, located in northeastern Arizona and parts of Colorado, New Mexico and Utah, contains homes of these ancient cliff dwellers. The Anasazi people made these homes in shallow natural caves along the towering canyon walls. These cliff dwellings were protected from weather and enemies. No one could attack the homes from above. And if anyone approached from below, the Anasazi could easily see them coming.

⇐ The sun has turned the soil of the cliff dwellings in Canyon de Chelly a deep red.

SCIENTISTS AND CANYONS

Scientists who study rocks and canyons are called *geologists.* By looking at canyon walls, geologists can see layers and layers of rock, much like the layers in a slice of cake. Many canyons have layers of mudstone, sandstone, and limestone that were laid down under the ocean millions of years ago. These kinds of rocks are called sedimentary rock. When they study canyon walls, geologists know the oldest layers are at the bottom and the youngest are at the top. By looking at these layers, the geologists can learn more about how the canyon formed—and about how the earth itself formed.

⇐ **Rock layers are easily seen at the Castle in Capitol Reef National Park, Utah.**

Canyon walls often contain traces of ancient plants and animals that have turned to rock. These traces are called *fossils*, and the scientists who study them are called *paleontologists*. By looking at the fossils in canyon walls, paleontologists can learn what plants and animals lived there at different times in the past. By cutting through countless layers of *sedimentary rock*, the Colorado River has revealed two billion years of history in the walls of the Grand Canyon.

Each layer of rock gets older as you go down into the Grand Canyon. ⇒

A WORLD OF WONDER

Canyons have been created over millions of years, eroded piece by tiny piece. They provide a look into the history of the earth itself. They are often deep and full of shadows. But when the sun's rays strike them, they reveal a rainbow of colors. Whether you are fishing for trout, hiking down a zigzagging trail, plunging through a raging set of rapids, or peering down from the rim, canyons are a place of wonder.

⇐ **A "Jeep Tour" is the easy way to travel into Canyon del Muerto, Arizona.**

INDEX

GLOSSARY

erosion (ee-ROH-zhun)
The way in which water wears its way through rock, one tiny piece at a time. Canyons are formed by erosion.

fossils (FOSS-ills)
Remains of ancient plants and animals that have been turned to rock. Fossils are often exposed in the rocks of canyon walls.

geologists (gee-OLL-oh-jists)
Scientists who study rocks. Geologists can learn about the earth's history by looking at the rocks of canyon walls.

paleontologists (pay-lee-un-TALL-oh-jists)
Scientists who study fossils, the remains of ancient plants and animals. Paleontologists often study fossils exposed in canyon walls.

plateau (plah-TOH)
A broad, flat area of land that is higher than the land around it. Streams sometimes carve canyons through plateaus.

sedimentary rock (sed-i-MEN-tuh-ree rok)
Rock that formed from mud and sand laid down underwater millions of years ago. Canyon walls often expose layer upon layer of sedimentary rock.

submarine canyons (SUB-muh-REEN KAN-yuns)
Canyons that form underneath the ocean.